Annie Oakley

a retelling by Eric Blair

illustrated by Dianne Silverman

PICTURE WINDOW BOOKS

a capstone imprint

My First Classic Story is published by Picture Window Books
A Capstone Imprint
151 Good Counsel Drive, P.O. Box 669
Mankato, Minnesota 56002
www.capstonepub.com

Printed in the United States of America in Stevens Point, Wisconsin.
092010
005934WZS11

Library of Congress Cataloging-in-Publication Data
Blair, Eric.
Annie Oakley / retold by Eric Blair ; illustrated by Dianne Silverman.
p. cm. — (My first classic story)
ISBN 978-1-4048-6577-8 (library binding)
1. Oakley, Annie, 1860-1926—Juvenile literature. 2. Shooters of firearms—
United States—Biography—Juvenile literature.
3. Entertainers—United States—Biography—Juvenile literature.
I. Silverman, Dianne, ill. II. Title.
GV1157.O3B5218 2011
799.3092
[B 2 22]   2010030642

Art Director: Kay Fraser
Graphic Designer: Emily Harris
Production Specialist: Michelle Biedscheid

For generations, storytelling was the main form of entertainment. Some of the greatest stories were tall tales, or exaggerated stories that may or may not have been about real people.

Annie Oakley was born in 1860. Her real name was Phoebe Ann Mosey. She was a talented sharpshooter and became the first American female superstar. Annie died in 1926, but her legend lives on.

When little Annie Oakley was five, her father died.

Annie may have been tiny, but she had very good eyesight.

To help feed her family, Annie learned to shoot.

People bought the animals she shot.

Annie earned so much money that she
bought her mother a farm.

When Annie was only sixteen, she entered a shooting contest.

She would shoot against Frank Butler,
a famous marksman.

Frank laughed at the tiny girl, but
Annie shot all twenty-five targets.

Frank missed one. Frank lost the contest, but he won Annie's heart. Soon, they were married.

Frank and Annie did trick shooting at shows.

People came from all over to see Annie's skills.

One of Annie's sharp-shooting tricks was to shoot an apple off a dog's head.

17

Annie could also shoot backwards and hit moving targets.

She watched the targets in a mirror.

Another trick Annie liked was to shoot a dime tossed into the air.

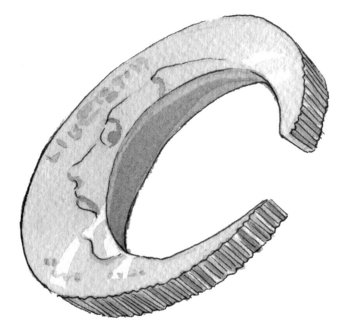

Sometimes, Annie even shot while riding a
horse!

Annie's favorite trick was to shoot
at a playing card.

She would shoot six holes into the
falling card before it hit the ground.

Annie had great tricks and great friends.
She was even friends with the famous
Sioux Indian Chief Sitting Bull.

He called her "Little Sure Shot."

After a while, Annie joined Buffalo Bill's
Wild West Show.

Annie Oakley became a star.

Annie toured the whole world.

The tours made Annie rich and famous.

Annie was generous with her money.
Once, she bought ice cream for all the kids
in Texas.

Annie Oakley was always tiny, but she had a huge heart.

The End